Big-Hearted Charlie Runs The Mile

By Krista Keating-Joseph

Illustrated by Phyllis Holmes

Printed in the United States of America

ISBN: 978-0-9972523-5-4

Published by
Legacies & Memories
St. Augustine, Florida

(888) 862-2754
www.LegaciesandMemoriesPublishing.com

Contact the Author
Website: www.KristaKeatingJoseph.com
E-mail: kkeatingjoseph@gmail.com

For my son, Charlie "C4"

For U.S. Navy SEALs
and their families

Big-Hearted Charlie Runs The Mile

He runs to school.

He runs through the park.

Charlie even runs to bed!

One day Charlie ran home from school with a piece of paper for his mom, asking him to join a track team.

12

"Mom, mom, can I join the team?

Please, can I join?" Charlie pleaded with his bright blue eyes.

"I know how much you love to run, Charlie, but it takes a lot of heart and dedication to be a member of a team," his mom replied. "I know mom, but I have a big heart," Charlie declared.

And she knew that he did!

15

The first day of practice was very hard.

He learned how to stretch his legs
and how to move his arms.

Charlie went to practice every day. He met other children who loved to run, too!

"Well, Charlie, I think you're ready for our first track meet.

Here's your uniform," said the coach.

Charlie was so excited! He lined up his shoes and even wore his uniform to bed!

He arose with the sun. For breakfast, he ate a small slice of toast and drank tea so he wouldn't get an upset stomach when he ran.

Charlie arrived at the track meet and started warming up with his team.

He checked in with the
starting-line official.

Charlie planned to run the one-mile race.
The mile was four laps around the track.

Charlie noticed other boys he was going to run against. They were from different teams and in his age group.

They were very, very BIG!

Charlie decided to run his best, no matter how little he was. Charlie was very big-hearted!

Finally, Charlie came around the last lap and could see the finish line. He felt bad that he was so far behind the other runners. 27

As he neared the finish line, the crowd
was standing and clapping just for him.
They were clapping for him
because he was LAST!

Charlie couldn't believe it. He felt like a winner, even though he was last.

Charlie ran across the finish line to his mom, who gave him the biggest hug.

"You never gave up Charlie and someday you will grow into that big heart of yours," his mom whispered. She was very proud of him.

The coach told Charlie, "You have the heart of a champion and you just have to work harder." That's just what Charlie did!

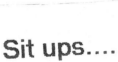

Sit ups....

Pull ups.....

Sit ups... Pull ups... Running farther...

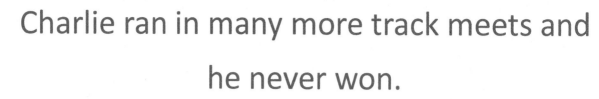

Charlie ran in many more track meets and he never won.

His mom asked him if he wanted to quit, but Charlie was determined to work harder.
Charlie would run farther and faster.
He would never give any excuses to his coach.
The coach knew Charlie had the biggest heart of any other runner.

Well, one day a very special thing happened.

Charlie's mom was right.

His coach was right.

Charlie grew into his Big Heart!

And the story is not over...

As Charlie became older and stronger, he decided to take on the biggest challenge. It was a challenge very few could accomplish.

Charlie became a U.S. Navy SEAL and his big heart saved the lives of many people. He received the Navy Cross, one of the highest honors in the Navy.

Acknowledgments

My Heroes

Special Thanks
My Husband Ron for Everything.
My Daughter Adele for Strength.
My Daughter Ali for Love.
My Son Billy for Faith and Fortitude.

Other Big-Hearted Thanks

Georganne Gillis; my parents, Bill and Phyllis Holmes; Vivian; Jerm; Abby; Aven; Taia; Brooke; Holly; Jordan; Collin; Nate; Colleen; Brian H.; James; Kyle; Alex; Pepper; Josh; Mr. M.; Beth W.; Lauren; Laurie; Renee; all "the cousins"; USO; Navy SEAL Foundation; City of Coronado, California; Our Lady Star of the Sea, Ponte Vedra Beach, Florida; Scottsdale Unified School District; USA Track & Field; The Patriot Guard Riders; All my wonderful friends for their constant support.

Contact Krista Keating-Joseph

Website: KristaKeatingJoseph.com
E-mail: kkeatingjoseph@gmail.com

43

CPSIA information can be obtained
at www.ICGtesting.com
Printed in the USA
LVOW06s1146220517
535406LV00026B/438/P